This edition published in 1993 by Mimosa Books, distributed by Outlet Book
Company, Inc., a Random House Company, 40 Engelhard Avenue, Avenel,
New Jersey 07001.

2 4 6 8 10 9 7 5 3 1

First published in 1993 by Grisewood & Dempsey Ltd.
Copyright © Grisewood & Dempsey Ltd. 1993

ISBN 1 85698 508 3

Printed and bound in Italy

THE THREE LITTLE PIGS
AND OTHER STORIES

MIMOSA
·BOOKS·

NEW YORK • AVENEL, NEW JERSEY

The Story of Persephone

This story is one of the tales that the ancient Greeks told about their gods. It is the story of Persephone, the lovely daughter of Demeter, Goddess of the Harvest.

Demeter traveled around the world with Persephone, visiting all the trees and plants that produce food. As she passed by, they grew and flourished, and their fruit ripened. On hot days as she walked through a field of corn, the husks would swell and the corn would turn golden. Whenever she visited orchards and vineyards, the apples, peaches, pears, and grapes would be sweet and ready to eat. Persephone would dance with joy to see how lovely the flowers looked when Demeter touched them.

One day, Persephone asked her mother is she could go and play with her friends on the mountainside. Demeter agreed, but warned her not to stray too far. While Demeter visited some valleys where the harvest was late, Persephone and her friends scrambled happily over the mountainside. They found many flowers growing in the mountain meadows and began to pick them to make garlands and chains. Farther and farther they wandered, until they were a long way from the valley where they had started.

Soon the meadows were shimmering in the hot midday sun. Persephone grew tired and dropped behind her friends. She sat

6

down on the grass to rest while she finished the garland she was making.

Suddenly there was a great crack and a roar. The side of the mountain seemed to split open and out galloped six great black horses, pulling a gleaming black chariot. Persephone was terrified and called out, "Mother, Mother, help me!" But even as she called, the man driving the chariot leaned out and swept Persephone up into the chariot. He pulled at the reins to turn the horses and they galloped back into the mountain. With another roar and a crash the gap closed, leaving no trace of what had happened.

Persephone's friends soon missed her and came back to look for her. They hunted everywhere and called and called, but there was no sign of her anywhere. At last they gave up and went back to tell Demeter.

Together they searched for hours up and down the mountain, but could find no trace of Persephone until, in the evening, they came upon a fading garland of flowers lying in the grass. Now Demeter knew that something dreadful must have happened to her daughter.

Something terrible had happened indeed. Persephone had been snatched by Hades, God of the Underworld. In his great black chariot, he drove her back to his palace of dark caverns deep inside the earth. The palace was full of beautiful things but Persephone was very unhappy there. She missed the sunlight and the flowers, and all the colors of the world she had known, and most of all she longed to see her mother. She was so unhappy that she refused to eat. She just sat in a corner, pining for her old home. Hades loved her and hoped to marry her, but Persephone time and again refused, saying that she wished only to return to the world above and her mother.

Meanwhile, Demeter continued to look for her daughter from

one end of the world to the other. While she searched, she gave no thought at all to the harvest. Everywhere the crops failed and the farmers watched in despair as their corn failed to ripen and their fruit withered on the trees.

Even Zeus, the King of the Gods, was worried. He did not wish to see the people on earth go hungry, so when Demeter asked him to help her find Persephone, he agreed to do what he could. His messengers soon came back with the information that she was with Hades in the Underworld. Zeus had no power over those who lived in the Underworld but there was a chance that Persephone might be saved. She had not yet eaten anything there and so had not yet become part of the Underworld. Each day Hades' servants bought her tempting dishes of exquisite fruit, but Persephone over and over again refused to touch them because she was so unhappy.

Zeus's messengers arrived in the Underworld once more and demanded that Persephone be returned to her mother. Hades knew that unless he could make her eat he would lose the lovely girl he wanted to marry. He ordered his servants to prepare a bowl of beautiful fruit and he himself carried it to Persephone. On the top he put a sweet-smelling pomegranate which he knew was her favorite fruit. Persephone, after much coaxing, reluctantly ate six seeds from the pomegranate, for she felt Hades had been kind to her and did not want to hurt his feelings. Then she turned her head

away and refused to eat any more, for the taste reminded her of the warm sunshine and the happy life that she missed so much. But Hades was triumphant, knowing that, because she had eaten food, she belonged forever to the Underworld.

Demeter was heartbroken. She grieved so much at the loss of her daughter that she had no heart to travel the earth as Goddess of the Harvest, and people began to grow hungry. Zeus was sorry for Demeter and for the people of the earth, so he sent his messengers to Hades once more to make a bargain: Persephone should spend six months of each year in the Underworld, one for each pomegranate seed she had eaten, but for the remaining six months she should return to the earth and join her mother.

And so it has been ever since. You will know when Persephone is in the Underworld with Hades as leaves fall and plants wither and die. During the six months we call Autumn and Winter Demeter is too unhappy to give any thought to the harvest. But when Persephone returns to the earth her mother is overjoyed and in her happiness makes the flowers open and new shoots spring from the ground. Crops flourish and fruit ripens to produce food. These six months when Persephone once more dances through the fields and orchards with her mother we call Spring and Summer.

The Little Jackal

There was once a little jackal who lived in the jungle. He was a greedy little jackal, and one of his favorite meals was fresh crabs from the river. One day he went down to the big river near his home and put his paw in the water to pull out a crab.

Snap! A large, lazy crocodile who had been lying in the water snapped his jaws and caught the jackal's paw. The little jackal did not cry out, although he was very frightened. Instead he laughed.

"Ha! Ha! That crocodile in the river thinks he has caught my paw, but the stupid animal does not realize he has snapped up a piece of wood and is holding it in his jaws."

The crocodile immediately opened his mouth for he did not want to be seen with a log of wood in his jaws. Quickly the little jackal danced away and called cheekily from a safe distance:

"I'll catch some crabs another day, Mr. Crocodile."

The crocodile lashed his tail with rage and resolved to catch the little jackal and eat him the next time he came to the river.

A week later, when his paw was healed, the jackal came back to the river to catch crabs. He did not want to be eaten by the crocodile, so he called out from a safe distance:

"I can't see any crabs lying on the bank. I'll have to dip my paw into the water near the edge," and he watched the river for a few minutes.

The crocodile thought, "Now is my chance to catch the jackal," and he swam close to the river bank.

When the little jackal saw the water move, he called out:

"Thank you, Mr. Crocodile. Now I know you are there, I'll come back another day."

The crocodile lashed his tail with rage until he stirred up the mud from the bottom of the river. He swore he would not let the little jackal trick him again.

The jackal could not stop thinking about the crabs, so a few days later he went down to the river again. He could not see the crocodile so he called out:

"I know crabs make bubbles in the water, so as soon as I see bubbles I'll dip my paw in and then I'll catch them easily."

When he heard this, the crocodile, who was lying just beneath the water started to blow bubbles as fast as he could. He was sure that the jackal would put his paw in where the bubbles were rising and Snap! This time he would have the little jackal.

But when the jackal saw the bubbles, he called out:

"Thank you, Mr. Crocodile, for showing me where you are. I'll come back another day for the crabs."

The crocodile was so angry at being tricked again that he waited till the jackal's back was turned, then he jumped out of the river and followed the jackal, determined to catch him and eat him this time.

Now the jackal, who was very hungry, made his way to the fig grove to eat some figs. By the time the crocodile arrived, he was having a lovely feast munching the ripe blue fruit, and licking his lips with pleasure.

The crocodile was exhausted by walking on land which he found was much more difficult than swimming in the river. "I am too tired to catch the jackal now," he said to himself. "But I'll set a

12

trap and catch him next time he comes for the figs."

The next day, the greedy jackal returned to the fig grove. He did love eating figs! To his surprise he saw a large and rather untidy pile of figs that had not been there before. "I wonder if my friend the crocodile has anything to do with this?" he said to himself, and he called out:

"What a lovely pile of figs! All I need to do is to see which figs wave in the breeze, for it is always the ripest and most delicious figs that wave in the breeze. I shall then know which ones to eat."

Of course the crocodile was buried under the pile of figs and when he heard this he smiled a big toothy crocodile smile. "All I have to do is to wriggle a bit," he thought. "When the jackal sees the figs move he will come and eat them and this time I will certainly catch him."

The little jackal watched as the crocodile wriggled under the pile of figs, and he laughed and laughed.

"Thank you, Mr. Crocodile," he said, "I'll come back another day when you are not here."

Now the crocodile was really in a rage, so he followed the little jackal to his house to catch him there. There was no one at home when the crocodile got there, but the crocodile thought, "I will wait here, and catch him when he comes home tonight."

He was too big to go through the gate, so he broke it and then he was too big to go through the door, so he smashed that. "Never mind," he said to himself. "I will eat the little jackal tonight whatever happens," and he lay in wait for the jackal in the jackal's little house.

14

When the jackal came home he saw the broken gate, and smashed door, and he said to himself, "I wonder if my friend the crocodile has anything to do with this?"

"Little house," he called out, "why haven't you said 'hello' to me as you do each night when I come home?"

The crocodile heard this, and thought he ought to make everything seem as normal as possible, so he shouted out:

"Hello little jackal!"

Then a wicked smile appeared on the jackal's face. He fetched some twigs and branches, piled them up outside his house, and set fire to it. As the house burned he called out:

"A roast crocodile is safer than a live crocodile! I shall go and build myself a new house by the river where I can catch all the crabs I want."

With that he skipped off to the river bank and for all I know he is still there today, eating crabs all day long, and laughing at the way he tricked the crocodile.

Goldilocks and the Three Bears

Once upon a time there were three bears who lived in a house in the forest. There was a great big father bear, a middle-sized mother bear, and a tiny little baby bear.

One morning, their breakfast porridge was too hot to eat, so they went for a walk in the forest. While they were out, a little girl called Goldilocks came through the trees and found their house. She knocked on the door and, as there was no answer, she pushed it open and went in.

In front of her was a table with three chairs, one great big chair, one middle-sized chair, and one tiny little chair. On the table were three bowls of porridge, one great big bowl, one middle-sized bowl, and one tiny little bowl – and three spoons.

Goldilocks was hungry, so she sat in the great big chair, picked up the biggest spoon and tried some of the porridge from the great big bowl. But the chair was far too big and hard, the spoon was too heavy, and the porridge too hot.

So Goldilocks went over to the middle-sized chair. But this chair was far too soft, and when she tried the porridge from the middle-sized bowl it was too cold. So she went over to the tiny little chair and picked up the smallest spoon and tried some of the porridge from the tiny little bowl.

This time it was neither too hot nor too cold. It was just right – and so delicious that Goldilocks ate it all up. But she was too heavy for the tiny little chair and it broke in pieces.

Then Goldilocks went upstairs, where she found three beds. There was a great big bed, a middle-sized bed, and a tiny little bed. First she lay down on the great big bed, but it was very big and far too hard. Next she lay down on the middle-sized bed, but that was far too soft. Then she lay down on the tiny little bed. It was neither too hard nor too soft. In fact, it felt just right, and Goldilocks fell fast asleep.

In a little while, the three bears came back from their walk in the forest.

Father Bear looked around, then roared in a great big growly voice,

"SOMEBODY HAS BEEN SITTING IN MY CHAIR!"

Mother Bear said in a quiet gentle voice,

"Somebody has been sitting in my chair!"

And Little Bear said in a small squeaky baby voice,

"*Somebody has been sitting in my chair, and has broken it!*"

Then Father Bear looked at his bowl of porridge and said in his great big growly voice,

"SOMEBODY HAS BEEN EATING MY PORRIDGE!"

Mother Bear looked at her bowl and said in her quiet gentle voice,

"Somebody has been eating my porridge!"

And Little Bear looked at his bowl and said in his small squeaky baby voice,

"*Somebody has been eating my porridge, and has eaten it all up!*"

Then the three bears went upstairs. Father Bear saw at once that his bed was untidy, and he said in his great big growly voice,

"SOMEBODY HAS BEEN SLEEPING IN MY BED!"

Mother Bear saw that her bed, too, had the bedclothes turned back, and she said in her quiet gentle voice,

"Somebody has been sleeping in my bed!"

And Little Bear looked at his bed, and he said in his small squeaky baby voice,

"*Somebody is sleeping in my bed, NOW!*"

He squeaked so loudly that Goldilocks woke up with a start. She jumped out of bed and ran down the stairs and out into the forest. And the three bears never saw her again.

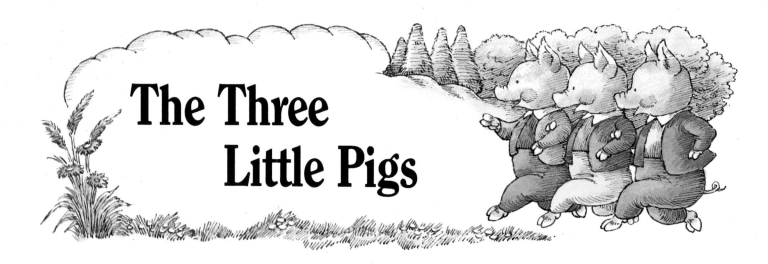

The Three Little Pigs

Once upon a time there were three little pigs. One day they set out from the farm where they had been born. They were going out into the world to make their fortune.

The first little pig met a man carrying some straw, and he asked him if he might have some to build himself a house.

"Of course, little pig," said the man. He gave the little pig a big bundle of straw, and the little pig built himself a lovely little house of golden straw.

By and by a big bad wolf came along and saw the new house. Feeling rather hungry and thinking he would like to eat a little pig for supper, he called out,

"Little pig, little pig, let me come in."
To which the little pig replied,
"No, no, by the hair of my chinny chin chin,
I'll not let you in."
So the wolf shouted crossly,
"Then I'll huff and I'll puff,
Till I blow your house in!"
And he huffed and he puffed until the house of straw fell in, and he ate the little pig for supper.

The second little pig was walking along the road when he met a man with a bundle of sticks. "Please, Sir," he said, "can you let me have some of those sticks so that I can build a house?"

"Of course," said the man, and he gave him a big pile of sticks. In no time at all, the little pig had built himself a lovely little house of sticks.

By and by, along came the same big bad wolf. When he saw another little pig, this time in a wooden house, he called out,

"Little pig, little pig, let me come in."

To which the little pig replied,
 "No, no, by the hair of my chinny chin chin,
 I'll not let you in."
So the wolf shouted,
 "Then I'll huff and I'll puff,
 Till I blow your house in!"
And he huffed and he puffed and he huffed and he puffed until the house of sticks fell in, and he gobbled up the little pig.
 The third little pig met a man with a cartload of bricks.

"Please, Sir, can I have some bricks to build myself a house?" he asked, and when the man had given him some, he built himself a lovely little brick house.

By and by the big bad wolf came along, and licked his lips as he thought about the third little pig. He called out,

"Little pig, little pig, let me come in."
And the little pig replied,

"No, no, by the hair of my chinny chin chin,
I'll not let you in."

So the wolf shouted,

"Then I'll huff and I'll puff,

Till I blow your house in!"

And the wolf huffed and he puffed, and he huffed and he puffed, and he HUFFED again and he PUFFED again, but still the house, which had been so well built with bricks, did not fall in.

The wolf went away to think how he could trick the little pig. He came back and called through the window of the brick house,

"Little pig, there are some juicy turnips in the farmer's field. Shall we go there tomorrow morning at six o'clock and get some?"

The little pig thought this was a good idea, as he was fond of turnips, but he went at five o'clock, not six o'clock, and collected all the turnips he needed before the wolf arrived.

The wolf was furious, but he soon thought of another trick. He told the little pig about the apples in the farmer's orchard, and

suggested they both went to get some at five o'clock the next morning. The little pig agreed, and went, as before, an hour earlier. But this time the wolf came early too and arrived while the little pig was still in the apple tree. The little pig pretended to be pleased to see him and threw an apple down to the wolf. While the wolf was picking it up, the little pig jumped down from the tree and got into a barrel. He rolled quickly down the hill inside this barrel and rushed into his house of bricks.

The wolf was furious that the little pig had got the better of him again, and chased him in the barrel back to his house. When he got there, he climbed onto the roof, intending to come down the chimney and catch the little pig that way. But the little pig was waiting for him with a large cauldron of boiling water on the fire. The wolf came down the chimney and fell into the cauldron with a big SPLASH, and the little pig quickly put the lid on it.

The wicked wolf was never seen again, and the little pig lived happily in his house of bricks for many years.